I0456288

BLACK IS MY HEART

Elise Noble

Published by Undercover Publishing Limited

Copyright © 2018 Elise Noble

v3

ISBN: 978-1-910954-84-3

Edited by Nikki Mentges, NAM Editorial

Cover design by Sapphire Designs

www.undercover-publishing.com

www.elise-noble.com

Fate decides who comes into your life.
Your heart decides who stays.

CHAPTER 1

EVER HEAR ABOUT the time an assassin got stuck in a closet while a sitting congressman got screwed to death by a pseudo-hooker on the other side of the door? Let me tell you, it was fucking awkward.

And totally not my fault. Not this time.

No, the blame for that little adventure lay squarely with Ahmedeen al-Shabari, a Middle Eastern terrorist who had trouble telling his red wire from his blue wire. Because if he hadn't accidentally blown himself up one fateful day in April, I'd have been kicking around in Afghanistan, topping up my tan and trying to avoid food poisoning instead of cursing out my laptop when Daniela di Grassi walked past my office.

"What's up?" she asked from the doorway.

"The damn E key just fell off. Who built this piece of crap?"

"Some twelve-year-old kid earning a buck an hour, probably."

For over a decade now, Dan had been one of my best friends, my colleague, and my partner in crime. We both worked at Blackwood Security, the company I owned along with my husband and two others, but while Dan was number two in the investigations division, I headed up Special Projects, which basically meant I dealt with all the shit nobody else wanted to touch.

"He was overpaid."

"Stop being such a bitch. What's put you in this charming mood?"

Boredom. "I've been stuck here for three days. Meetings, meetings, and more meetings."

"Well, you're in luck. I've got the perfect fix."

Her fake cheerfulness didn't fill me with joy. "Oh?" Then I spotted the folder under her arm. "The Carmody kidnapping?"

Seven-year-old Mila Carmody had disappeared nine months ago, snatched from her bed in the middle of the night in every parent's worst nightmare. No witnesses, no ransom demands, and no sign of the little girl despite a manhunt involving half the cops in Virginia plus the FBI. The only clue was a tiny speck of blood on the catch of Mila's window, a speck that didn't belong to her or anybody else in the nationwide DNA databases.

Mila's family had hired us three months ago to do a case review, but despite Dan's impressive solve rate, she'd been as stumped as everybody else. Had there been a breakthrough?

Dan shook her head. "Nope. Carmody's still keeping me awake at night, but that's not it. Remember when Rhonda Swanson-Clements came in the other day?"

How could I forget? Two weeks ago, the wife of Paul Clements, our esteemed Representative for the seventh district of Virginia, had insisted on a last-minute, out-of-hours meeting, and when I'd offered her a coffee as I passed her waiting in reception, she'd given me a disgusted look when I told her we didn't have half-and-half. Or at least, her nose had wrinkled. Her forehead was frozen in place by a thousand bucks' worth of Botox.

"Yeah, I remember. She was referred over by Rhodes, Holden and Maxwell?"

The law firm we had on retainer, which also handled a number of high-profile clients. I'd noticed the connection on our case log, but I hadn't read the details.

"Yup, by her freshly appointed divorce attorney."

One of the golden couples of politics was splitting? I suppose I wasn't hugely surprised, seeing as Congressman Clements was a world-class dick. And Rhonda was well-known in her own right—the heiress to a property fortune, she'd kept herself on the map by campaigning for children's literacy and donating books to schools all over America.

"Who dumped who?"

"She ditched him. She's had—and I quote—enough of his foolin' around."

"Why now? Haven't they been married for twenty years?"

"Twenty-five. Apparently, her new therapist's helped her to see that there's more to life than being a doormat."

Everybody had a fucking therapist nowadays. You know what I saw on TV the other day? A pet counsellor. For only a hundred and twenty dollars an hour, she'd tell you how your four-legged friend felt unloved because you went out to work all day in order to pay for its session with a charlatan.

"I could have told her that for free."

"Yeah, well, the therapist's a guy. Young, hot in a preppy kinda way according to the picture on his website, and fifty bucks says she's screwing him."

"What makes you think that?"

"Whenever she mentioned his name, her eyes flicked up to the left and went all dreamy."

Eyes to the left meant she was remembering, and Dan was good at reading people. Still, if Rhonda wanted to play cougar, that was her business, not ours.

"Where do we come in?"

"The marital fortune was mostly hers, and the prenup says Paul Clements is entitled to three million bucks for every year of marriage unless he was unfaithful."

"And then?"

"Then he gets squat."

"Let me guess—she wants us to find proof of his infidelity."

"Got it in one. Except it's proving to be harder than I thought. Clements is careful. Rhonda already hired one PI, and all he found out was that the dude liked to go for long, meaningless drives in the countryside."

"She's sure he's cheating?"

"He comes home freshly showered, and he's not a man who goes to the gym in the evening."

That I could believe. The man had the physique of a marshmallow. "But that's hardly conclusive."

"She also found Viagra in his jacket pocket, and he doesn't use it with her."

"So, why do you need me?"

"Because the court date's in nine days, and I haven't found what we need. Just one picture with a woman, but when the lawyers got into a game of show-and-tell, Clements claimed she was a social-media consultant."

"What, for his features on Pornhub?"

Dan shrugged. "I need to dig up something conclusive."

"Catch him in the act, you mean? That's difficult to do legally. It won't be admissible in court."

"I don't think Rhonda cares about that. She wants to send it to celebgossip.com."

Oh, what a shame.

As a rule, I didn't like politicians of any persuasion, but in a moment of weakness, I'd dated a senator a few years ago, and he'd spent many evenings bitching about Clements when the self-centred prick torpedoed a bill to improve healthcare provisions for kids across the country. The fact that Clements's campaign was in part funded by three insurance providers hadn't escaped my notice.

"Couldn't happen to a nicer guy."

"It's not gonna happen to anyone if I can't find some actual evidence."

Dammit, I hated cheating-spouse cases. The petty squabbling made me want to punch something—or rather, someone—and worse, the endless screwing around reminded me that my own dry spell was fast heading for double figures. What's that you say? But you're married? Well, yes, I was, but it was basically a marriage of convenience. Or at least, it had started out that way one drunken night when I tied the knot with my boss in Vegas. I didn't even like him much at the time. It was only afterwards that I fell in love with him, which was a huge fucking mistake because he didn't feel the same way. Every relationship I'd ever attempted had fallen apart, and since my sometimes-fuck buddy was working in Iraq or Afghanistan or some other godforsaken sandpit, I'd gone beyond frustrated and all the way to dusting cobwebs off my clitoris. At that point in time, I had more vibrators than I had guns, and I had a *lot* of guns.

But because I really couldn't stand Congressman Clements, I'd suck it up and help a girl out.

"There must be something we can use."

"Rumour has it he books girls through the Kerrane Agency. And when I say rumour, I mean Mack hacked in and found an account with his assistant's phone number and a false name."

Ah, the Kerrane Agency. Washington, DC's most exclusive provider of female companionship, as their website put it, whose motto was literally "You don't pay for sex. You pay for discretion." The girls there were covered by hefty NDAs, they'd happily play along with elaborate cover stories, and they got paid enough that bribery was difficult. A year with Kerrane could set a college girl up for life, and some went on to treat it as a career.

"Tricky."

"I need to get to a Kerrane girl," Dan said. "Any ideas?"

"None of them'll want to go up against Clements. He's got seventy-five million reasons to accuse a girl of lying and drag her name through the mud."

"And he also has a well-paid assistant set up to take the fall if we get too close."

"If only he put as much effort into advocating for his constituents as he does into getting laid."

"America would be a better place, right? Speaking of getting laid, how's the—"

"Shut up."

"I don't understand how you've let the whole

celibacy thing go on for so long."

"Because I'm waiting for Mr. Right."

"But who knows how long that'll take? It's not like you put any effort into looking. When was the last time you went on an actual date?"

"Define 'date.'"

"Something more romantic than fucking Jed Harker in the second-floor restroom."

"You know about that?"

"Sweetie, Malachi saw the two of you go in there. *Everybody* knows."

Including my husband, no doubt. Fuck. Damn Mal and his penchant for gossip. In a past life, he was one of those old ladies who loved to sit out on the porch all day, drinking iced tea and knitting while they dissected the neighbourhood goings-on in minute detail.

"Jed had to catch a flight," I muttered. "We were in a hurry."

"Jed isn't the only man out there with working equipment. Why not have Mr. Right Now while you wait around for Mr. Right?"

"How about getting back onto the subject of work? You know, that thing we pay you for?"

"Should I bow down to the Queen Bitch as well?"

"If you like."

She kicked me in the shin instead. "Okay, work. Find me a Kerrane girl who'll talk. You know you love a challenge, my Queen."

True, although I preferred breaking and entering or finding ways to kill particularly irritating terrorists. But you know what I never did?

Gave up.

I *never* gave up. Every problem had a solution even

if it wasn't the most obvious one.

"You'll owe me for this."

"Sure. I'll buy you another vibe."

I grabbed the nearest thing off my desk and lobbed it at her, but she ducked, and the screen on my stupid phone shattered as it hit the glass wall of my office.

"Fuck you."

"I don't think so, sweetie. I only do men."

Grrrrr.

CHAPTER 2

TICK, TICK, TICK...

The Kerrane girls were tough nuts to crack. In an ideal world, I'd play the long game, but three days had passed, and time was running out. With help from Mack and Dan, I'd identified four likely candidates I could push for information, then narrowed it down to the one most likely to give me what I wanted. A sweet college graduate in her late twenties named Celina, who told acquaintances a trust fund paid for her three-bedroom townhouse when she'd grown up in a trailer park in Illinois. Better still, Celina had a prescription drug habit that needed feeding, and she also happened to be roommates with Clements's "social-media consultant." Girls liked to talk, to each other at least. Look at yours truly—I did enough illegal shit to get locked up for eternity if the wrong people ever caught me, but I always bitched about it over cocktails with Dan and Mack because a problem shared is a problem thirded. If the shit hit the fan, they'd be my cellmates anyway. So, the day before yesterday, I'd joined the same gym as Celina, and when I accidentally-on-purpose ended up on the treadmill next to her, she'd raved about this afternoon's hot yoga class. Guess what I was doing later?

A hand landed on my shoulder, and I resisted the

urge to lean into my husband's touch as he loomed over me. Most people didn't have that problem—since he stood at six feet seven of pure muscle and generally looked a bit threatening, mere mortals tended to take a couple of paces back and swallow hard.

"Coffee, Diamond?"

"We've been married for eleven years and you still have to ask that?"

He moved to the espresso machine on the far side of the kitchen and added freshly ground beans while I took a bite out of the English muffin our housekeeper had set in front of me. Wholemeal, of course. My nutritionist had banned refined grains this week because his one joy in life was making me miserable.

"What are your plans for today?" my husband asked. "Do you need a ride to the office?"

"I have a torture session in half an hour." Otherwise known as part two of a gym date with Alex, my personal trainer. "Then I'm gonna fit in some target practice, and this afternoon, I get to strip half-naked and twist myself into a pretzel."

He raised one dark eyebrow. "Tell me more."

"I'm researching the Kerrane Agency."

"Dare I ask why?"

"I'm considering a career change."

Now I earned an eye roll, which was about as expressive as he got. "You're not compliant enough for that."

"I can do compliant if it means I don't have to get up at six to have the shit kicked out of me."

"If it's any consolation, Alex was limping on his way to the steam room." That did make me feel a tiny bit better. "Tell me about Kerrane."

"Divorce case. We need to catch a politician with his pants down."

"Tricky. How long do you have?"

"Six days. Which is why I'm going to yoga with a blonde named Celina."

"Forget it. She won't talk."

"I'm desperate, okay?"

"So the rumours are true?"

"Shut up. Bad enough that—" Wait, wait, wait... "Hey, how do you know that Celina won't talk?"

He gave a tiny, one-shouldered shrug and stepped backwards. Out of range.

"Because I'm a good judge of character."

A chill ran through me. I knew he had to get his kicks somehow, but we'd never discussed the logistics, and I'd always kind of figured he did the same as Dan and picked up strangers in the nightclub I owned.

"And when exactly did you judge hers?"

"Do you really want to talk about this?"

Not in the slightest. "You started it."

"Fine."

He tensed his jaw. Released it. My husband was a man who never showed emotion, but I'd known him long enough to pick up on his tells, and he absolutely didn't want to be having this chat. But I had a case to close, so tough luck.

"I met Celina after the Diana episode. Diana's clinginess was..." He paused for a moment, taking time to think the way he always did. "Unsettling. I wanted an arrangement where the boundaries were clearly defined."

Hearing that admission was a thousand times worse than anything Alex could have delivered, and I felt a ridiculous urge to claw Celina's pretty blue eyes out. Even though I had no right to feel that way. My husband had taken me from nothing and given me everything I wanted except himself, and apart from one drunken mistake, he'd never crossed the line between what we had and what I craved.

His position was clear. I didn't like it, but I had to live with it. *Clang, clang, clang*. My armour slotted back into place, and I forced a neutral expression onto my face.

"And during this arrangement, did you learn anything that could help our case?"

"Not from Celina, but one of the other girls"—oh, this just got better and better—"owes me a favour. Seems like the right time to call it in." His voice softened infinitesimally. "Tanya. I never spent the night with her. She was a friend of Celina's, and she was having trouble with an asshole in her building."

The coffee machine beeped, and two seconds later, I had a double espresso in front of me. Which I scalded my tongue on. Remind me again why I got out of bed today?

"I need to get back to the gym," I muttered. "Call me if you get anything, yeah?"

I shoved my chair back and stood, leaving three-quarters of a muffin and most of the coffee behind. My appetite had vanished, along with my last forlorn hope of having a normal, healthy relationship. What man in his right mind would want to date an assassin, anyway? I'd tried a former Navy SEAL, a fellow hitman, the ex-senator, a French spy, an FBI agent, and a CIA manwhore, but something always went wrong. Perhaps I should've forgotten the call-girl idea and become a nun instead.

How did I end up as an assassin? Well, it was a dirty job, but somebody had to do it. Just like modern society couldn't function properly without plumbers and garbage collectors and undertakers, the world wouldn't turn quite so smoothly without a quiet few removing the cancerous scum that festered in quiet corners before they got out of control. Why go? Because thirteen years ago, I ran into a man in the backstreets of London who discovered I had a talent for it.

And now here I was.

"I thought your next session with Alex wasn't for a half hour?" my husband said.

"Don't want to be late."

"You're always late."

"And you always nag me for it."

"Diamond..."

"See you later."

If I'd actually had a résumé, running away from my problems would have been somewhere near the top of the skills section, below making murder look like an accident and above talking my way out of speeding tickets. I'd had plenty of practice at all three over the years. Now, at twenty-nine years old, I'd got to a place where I couldn't quite call myself happy, but I was comfortable with who—and what—I'd become.

Revelations like this morning's fed the monster that lurked under the surface of my psyche. Left me twitchy and stoked my biggest fear—the fear that I'd lose my husband. Our relationship might not have been conventional, but he was my rock, my confidant, and my soulmate. I could do the impossible with him by my side, but without him? I never wanted to find out.

CHAPTER 3

"I THOUGHT YOU were going to yoga this afternoon?" Dan asked. Five p.m., and I was sitting in the visitors' chair opposite her desk, flicking my favourite knife open and closed. *Snick. Click. Snick. Click. Snick. Click.*

"Change of plan."

"Another job?"

No, I just didn't feel like being outdone by Celina in the perkiness stakes.

"A new lead."

"What kind of lead? I'm juggling thirty cases, and Rhonda's called me six times already today. Okay, so one of those calls was asking my opinion on that new wine bar by Main Street Station, but the rest were all demanding updates on our progress. Or rather, the lack of it."

"Just keep her calm."

"Do you really have something concrete? Because I've got zilch apart from a strong suspicion that Paul Clements is actually a slug in a skin onesie."

"Keep the faith, sister."

Even if I struggled with that myself. Why the hell hadn't my husband called yet?

Speak of the devil, my phone buzzed. Well, he was more like the Grim Reaper, since he'd taught me most of what I knew about the art of death. I hurried out of

Dan's office and into my own, then pressed the phone against my ear.

"Tell me you've got something."

"I've got something."

"Well? What is it?"

"A chocolate gateau from Claude's. Mrs. Fairfax is making coq au vin, and I thought we could have dinner together."

"What about the case?"

"We'll talk over dinner."

Damn, he was good at this game. Since he had two things I wanted—information and cake—he knew I couldn't make an excuse and avoid him. Well played, Mr. Black. Well played. In our world, information was currency, and if you spent it wisely, you could buy power.

"I'll be home in twenty minutes."

"You're in the office, and that's half an hour away."

"Have you been tracking my phone again?"

"We've been married for eleven years and you still have to ask that?"

"Asshole. Twenty minutes, and you'd better have a glass of wine waiting."

The engine of my Dodge Viper roared as I pushed it into the bends. A surprise birthday gift, the car had allowed me to shave almost two minutes off my best time to the office with its 8.3-litre engine and nice fat tyres, so I skidded into the driveway at home in only nineteen minutes with no traffic citations and just a hint of burning rubber.

My chocolate cake was waiting for me in the dining room of the larger of our two Virginia houses, as was my husband, and I took a swallow from my glass of white and a seat at one end of the table, in that order. I rarely drank, but if any night called for alcohol, it was this one. I glanced at the label on the bottle. Montes Blackwood vineyard, Portugal. Blackwood Hills. Did we own that? I was pretty sure we owned that.

Usually, we ate in the kitchen, but since we operated something of an open-house policy, friends often dropped by unannounced. The fact that my beloved had selected the vast dining room with its wood panelling and ornate velvet curtains told me he wanted to keep tonight's conversation between the two of us.

"You've kept me waiting for long enough," I said. "Speak."

"Does your car have any tread left on the tyres?"

"Just spill already."

"Patience, Diamond." He sipped his own wine. "Tanya wasn't particularly keen to talk, but I gave my word that her name would stay out of it."

"No problem."

"We're lucky she doesn't like Paul Clements either. Apparently, he lets the woman do all the work."

A faint smirk told me what my husband thought of that idea, and unwanted heat pooled between my legs. The wine bottle was within reach, so I poured myself another glass, even though what I really wanted to do was tip the contents of the ice bucket over my head.

"I don't understand what Rhonda ever saw in him."

"He's good at manipulating people. With the Kerrane girls, he insists they come dressed in business attire, prepared for a bullshit meeting if any paparazzi are sniffing around."

"Where do they hook up? Dan got a picture of him at a restaurant with one woman, but that came to nothing."

"There's a parking garage beside the Fairchild Hotel, and Clements has two spaces reserved on the third floor. Clements's assistant parks in one, and when the girl arrives, he checks her over for electronics then drives her to meet the boss. She has to leave her purse in the trunk."

"Wow. Paranoid or what?"

"Justifiably so, wouldn't you say?"

"I guess. Where do they go after that?"

"Clements owns half a dozen apartment buildings. And when I say owns, I mean they're in his name, but he bought the entire portfolio with his wife's money. Call it a retirement project. He borrows an empty unit whenever the need arises—doesn't take long, by all accounts."

I knew the first part, but not the second or the third. "Dan's file says he visits the building managers for weekly catch-up meetings. I bet he uses them as a cover."

"You have to give the man credit for thinking this through."

"We're still taking him down."

"I don't doubt that for a second, Diamond."

But it wouldn't be easy. I blew out a long breath, thinking. "So the hooker's never alone in the apartment, we can't bug it in advance because we don't know which one he'll use, and we can't hide a recording device in a purse either. Does he have a regular girl? If we could get to her..."

A shake of the head nixed that idea. "He told Tanya that variety is the spice of life."

What a great attitude to have in a supposedly monogamous relationship.

"Dan's gonna be thrilled about this."

"You both relish a challenge."

He disarmed me with a smile, the one he never showed outside the privacy of our own home, and I shoved all the thoughts of politicians and hookers and photographic ammunition to one side to enjoy the evening for what it was—dinner with my husband. My best friend.

I managed a smile of my own. "Is dinner in the oven? I'll bring it through."

"No, you'll sit and enjoy your wine. I'll get dinner."

My gaze lingered on his ass as he headed out the door, tightly sculpted muscle that put Michelangelo's *David* to shame. Fuck. My insides liquefied, and I slid a few inches lower on my fancy leather seat.

This man would be the death of me.

An hour later, after I'd got through most of the bottle of wine and three-quarters of the cake—because Mr. Health Freak opted for only a small slice plus a freaking apple—I'd mostly repressed the difficulties of the Clements case in favour of planning a rock-climbing trip in mangled Japanese. Our company would be opening an office in Tokyo soon, and for the past few months, we'd been learning the basics of the language so we didn't need to rely on translators the whole time. But Japanese wasn't the easiest thing in the world to master.

"What did you just say?" I asked.

"I said I'd come to meet you at the office."

"No, you said you'd come to assassinate me at the office."

"Are you sure?"

"Yup. You said *ansatsu* when you meant *aisatsu*."

He grinned. "Some days, *ansatsu* seems like the better idea."

"Keep that up, and perhaps I *will* change my career. I wonder if Kerrane's hiring?"

"At least if we had a professional on the inside, it would make collecting dirt on politicians easier." The last traces of my husband's smile disappeared, leaving only a frown. "Diamond, I haven't used Kerrane's services recently. Not for years. I just wanted you to know that."

He kept speaking, odd for a man who was as economical with words as he was with bullets, but the rest of the conversation barely registered because the first part of his comment had fired off a bunch of synapses in my brain.

"That's it!"

"Sorry?"

"Why are we spending all this time trying to net an informant when we can put a chunk of juicy bait on the hook and reel in the big fish ourselves?"

"What's with the fishing analogies?"

"I couldn't sleep last night, and I ended up watching *River Monsters* until the early hours." My chair scraped across the floor as I pushed it back. Once on my feet, I clutched at the edge of the table and willed the room to stop swaying because I felt kind of sick. "I need to make a phone call."

I lurched through the door, stumbling towards the

stairs as my husband's voice echoed faintly along the hallway behind me.

"Diamond, you're *not* using yourself as bait."

CHAPTER 4

"IT'S ME."

SNOW groaned softly in my ear. Snow wasn't her real name, of course, just like mine wasn't Diamond or Valkyrie or Cinders or any of the other hundred things I answered to.

"It's three o'clock in the morning."

"Where are you?"

"Marrakesh." Dammit, I'd been hoping she was somewhere a little closer. "In a shitty hotel near the airport. My flight to JFK got cancelled."

"Thank fuck for that. Not that your flight got canned, but that you're back coming. I mean, coming back."

"Have you been drinking? You sound weird."

"Hmm, am I drunk? I think so. Yes."

"Special occasion?"

"Just trying to block out the job from hell, which, by the way, I desperately need your help with."

Snow snorted out a laugh. "You're not really selling it."

"I can send a plane for you. Shall I send a plane?" I tapped away at the nearest keyboard in the first-floor operations room, which functioned as a backup control room for our company as well as a glorified home office. The bigger of our two jets was in England, my home country, and four hours from Morocco. "Tell me you've got a couple of days free?"

"Stop. Start from the beginning, okay?"

I guess I should probably mention at this point that Snow was in the same line of business as me. She was also a friend. A good friend. The kind of friend that came along once or twice in a lifetime, one of those rare people I just clicked with, and even though months could pass without us speaking, we could pick up exactly where we left off.

And almost as important, she had exactly the skills I needed right now. While I was a crack shot, good with a knife, and practiced in the art of trickery, Snow masqueraded as a succubus when she wasn't busy poisoning people. Me? I didn't mind teaming up with her for the occasional honeytrap, but I drew the line at actual sex with the targets. Snow didn't have any lines. Her services were always in demand with the powers that be, but she'd do me a favour if she had the time, just like I'd help her out in a pinch.

"So, there's a guy..." I gave her a quick rundown on Congressman Clements, careful not to mention any names or particulars. Even though we both used secure phones, technology wasn't infallible, and you never knew who was listening. We'd worked together for long enough that Snow understood what I was saying without me spelling it out. "And we have a deadline. Six days."

"I've got five before my next job starts."

Thank goodness. That was tight, but did I mention I specialised in achieving the downright difficult?

"How soon can you get back?"

"My flight leaves in five hours."

"I'll send a jet to JFK to pick you up."

And then I'd begin scheming in earnest. I had my team and I had my goal—now all I needed to do was work out the logistics. Number one, get the right electronics. Nate, another of our business partners, would take care of that for me. When he wasn't busy plotting somebody's death, he loved to tinker in his basement lab back at headquarters. Number two, borrow a car or three. We wouldn't want to use vehicles that could be traced back to us. Then we'd need to beef up the surveillance team on Clements and put another on his assistant. Get somebody in place to watch the parking garage. We'd have to find the right clothes, and Snow would want to change her appearance if she was gonna appear on camera...

A shadow darkened the doorway as I grabbed a notepad and pen, and my husband glided towards me.

"What are you doing, Diamond?"

"Working." I turned my attention back to Snow. "Can you message me your flight details?"

"You owe me dessert for this."

"Anything you want."

"Waffles. No ice cream."

I mentally added a trip to Claude's onto my to-do list. The best French restaurant in Richmond, and I was a regular customer. Yes, waffles were Belgian, but Claude would make me anything if I asked nicely, and he'd make it to perfection.

"They'll be waiting. See you tomorrow."

My husband stared down at me. "Do I want to know?"

"Probably not." A giggle escaped, because alcohol. "Snow's coming. I need to organise a flight for her."

"No, you need to get some sleep."

"I'm fine."

"Your eyes are focusing in two different directions, and you're trying to write with the pen cap on."

"But—"

"Bed." He didn't give me a chance to argue, just wheeled my chair back and plucked me out of it, bridal-style. "I'll do whatever needs to be done tonight."

Nestled in his arms, the fight went out of me. Today had been horrible in so many ways, but as the moon rose, I ended up exactly where I wanted to be—in my husband's arms, feeling the steady thump of his heartbeat against my chest.

"Okay. I'll go to bed."

CHAPTER 5

"ARE YOU SURE that's short enough? She doesn't look very slutty."

Bradley, my assistant, appraised Snow as she tugged the hem of her knee-length black skirt down over her ass, and she gave him an exasperated look.

"I have to pass as a businesswoman."

"She's not Julia Roberts in *Pretty Woman*," I told him.

Mack glanced up from her laptop. "No, that's Dan."

Dan wasn't playing a prostitute tonight, but that hadn't stopped her from wearing a leather skirt that was more of a belt. And Bradley was right in his observation, though I'd never admit it because his ego was quite big enough, thank you. Snow looked nothing like a lady of the night. No, she had more of an executive-assistant vibe going on, which was perfect for this evening's excursion. She'd put her mask on now. Stoic resignation, which would turn into a convincing smile when Clements came near. In some ways, I envied her ability to block out her feelings. My shitty childhood had left me inherently suspicious, sometimes bolshy, sometimes evasive, and unless I knew a man well, he'd better keep his hands off unless he wanted his nose broken. Snow, on the other hand, dealt with years of abuse by simply refusing to feel at all. That trait, combined with Oscar-worthy acting skills, had made her a rich woman. A *very* rich woman. She was two years younger than me, and if she chose, she'd never have to work another day in her life. But one thing everybody in the room had in common was that we loved the thrill of the chase.

"I'm no Vivian," Dan said. "I don't need a man to pay my way."

"And if you drove a Lotus, you'd crash it," I pointed out.

"Hey, you'll be grateful for my skills behind the wheel later."

"Quit with the bickering," Bradley grumbled, fastening a gold bracelet around Snow's wrist before he turned his attention to me. "And what are you wearing? Is that polyester?"

"I need to be forgettable."

"Couldn't you add a tiny bit of colour?"

My glare gave him his answer.

"Honestly, you're so unadventurous."

And that was exactly how I liked it, at least in terms of attire. Dull and unmemorable when the need arose, I wore my own mask every time I left the sanctuary of my home turf. I could be a real-estate agent or a waitress or a scientist or a dancer, and although I fought like a tiger, my spirit animal was a chameleon.

But I couldn't afford to dwell on the past today. No, I had to tuck all those emotions away and focus on the task at hand. Put that cold veneer back on. The men on Capitol Hill called me the Ice Queen, but I rarely dressed in white. Despite Bradley's best efforts to introduce the entire fucking rainbow into my life, I stuck with shades of grey that reflected the shadows I lived my life in, and dark hues that matched my soul and my little black heart.

Tonight's plan was simple. One of the surveillance operatives following Perkins, Clements's assistant, had overheard him on the phone earlier, arranging a meet at the parking garage at nine p.m. All we had to do was intercept the girl and replace her with Snow. Because Snow's electronic goodies would get confiscated, I'd follow them to the evening's assignation and sneak in with a camera. Snow would do her thing, and *boom*—we'd have the photos we needed to make Rhonda Swanson-Clements seventy-five million bucks richer. Our fee wasn't bad either. Dan had negotiated one and a half percent if we solved the problem. Even split with Snow, that would buy a lot of cake.

"Clements is on the move," Dan said, tucking back her hair to reveal the earpiece that gave her a direct line to the surveillance teams. "Heading towards Fairmount."

Why didn't we just follow him and his Kerrane girl, you ask? Because trying to sneak into a high-rise apartment to film a dirty movie when neither of the stars was a willing participant in the plan added a layer of risk I didn't want to take. If there was a problem, Snow would cover for me and vice versa.

And there were always problems. No matter how well-planned a job was, we still had to factor in an appearance by Mr. Murphy of Murphy's Law fame. He loved to ride along and make our lives just a little bit more interesting. Like the time my gun jammed in the middle of a firefight in Iraq, or that moment an escaped dog almost blew a six-month-long operation when he sniffed out a surveillance operative, or the lightning strike on our plane in... Yeah, you get the picture.

Tonight, we were as ready as we could be. Earlier, we'd arranged the vehicles and licence plates we'd need —some ours, some "borrowed"—and we'd all either walked or driven through the parking garage to get an idea of the layout. Six storeys, two cameras per floor, plenty of dimly lit corners, and a security office at the front. Yesterday, we'd mapped out the locations of each of Clements's buildings and worked out the most suitable entrances and exits. The apartment blocks were middle-of-the-road. Utilitarian. Functional. Not slums but far from luxurious. CCTV covered the first-floor doors, and each had a supervisor who hung out in the lobby at odd times of day. Annoyingly unpredictable.

"Guess we should be leaving too, then," I said.

The prospect of seeing Mr. Clements buck naked didn't exactly fill me with joy, and the sooner it was over, the better.

We filed downstairs with Bradley still fussing around, spraying perfume and muttering about heel height and lipstick and looking good for the cameras. It didn't matter. Clements didn't have great eyesight, and whatever pictures we gave to Rhonda, they wouldn't show Snow's face.

"Got everything?" my husband asked as he walked past, dressed to party with a Colt M45 in his shoulder holster and three spare magazines clipped beside the knife on his belt.

Snow nodded. "Knife, condoms, GHB... Yes. Where are you going?"

"Off to rescue a teenage runaway from a crack den. The parents got threatened when they tried it themselves."

"You get all the good jobs," I grumbled.

"Want me to pick up dinner on my way home?"

Mrs. Fairfax had the day off, which meant we had to fend for ourselves. "Unless you'd rather I poisoned you with my cooking?"

"I don't mind making something," Snow offered.

He eyed her up and grimaced faintly. "Should I get pizza? Chinese? Mexican?"

"Yes."

"I'm not going to three fucking restaurants."

"Chinese," Dan said. "And make sure you get fortune cookies."

Or not. Last time, mine told me I'd get a big break in life, and two days later, I'd cracked a rib in a fistfight. What predictions would be revealed tonight? I wasn't sure I wanted to know.

CHAPTER 6

I SLOUCHED DOWN in the seat of my Ford Focus, waiting for a cue to move. Twenty minutes ago, Clements had strolled into one of his buildings, a sixteen-storey apartment block called The Wainscott. They all had pretentious names. Oppidan, King's Rest, Granville Place...

"Got a possible," Mack said from her position on the first floor of the parking garage. Usually, she stayed in the office, but we'd convinced her to come out and join in the fun tonight. "Brunette in a cherry-red Peugeot convertible. Pretty. I'm running the plates now."

Hurry up, hurry up, hurry up... With Clements's assistant parked on the third floor and Dan waiting in place one floor below in a Honda that had seen better days, we only had seconds to make a decision. Was this our target?

Fortunately, Mack didn't waste any time. "Hit it."

A moment later, I heard the *crunch* of metal and plastic that could only have been a minor car accident. When we assigned roles, Dan was the obvious choice for that part on account of she'd had so much practice at crashing.

Her voice came through loud and clear with just the right amount of panic. "Oh my gosh! I'm so sorry."

A stranger spoke, young-sounding and justifiably peeved. The call girl, no doubt. "Did you even look before you pulled out?"

"I thought I did, but my cat died this morning, and then my credit card got cloned, and my landlord's being a complete dick about the pipe that burst in my apartment, and I guess with all that I just got distracted."

A car engine purred, and I pictured Snow pulling out of her parking spot a few spaces along from Dan. Driving up the ramp. Slotting in neatly beside the assistant's Mercedes. Climbing out and putting her purse in the trunk. Standing slightly pissed while Perkins patted her down or wanded her or whatever he did to check she wasn't wearing a wire, then climbing into the passenger seat for the short trip to The Wainscott.

Confirmation came from one of our watchers two minutes later. "Snow's on the move."

Which meant it was time for me to get my arse in gear too. I slipped out of the car and strode down the street, walking with purpose because tourists rarely visited that part of Richmond. Earlier in the day, one of my team had wedged the fire door with a folded-up flyer, so I should be able to—

Dammit.

Either the fire escape got used as a thoroughfare, or the building supervisor did his job and checked things properly. None of which boded well for me, since I wanted to sneak inside without getting caught on candid camera in the lobby. Ah well, I still had fifteen minutes. Plenty of time to find another way in before Snow arrived, right?

"Slight technical hitch," I muttered into the microphone hidden in the button on my lapel.

"Oh?" Mack said.

"The fire door's a no-go."

"Do you need backup? Heidi's taking Dan out for coffee, but I could get Dan to make an excuse."

"Heidi?"

"The call girl. When Perkins wasn't there, she and Dan got talking. Shall I radio through?"

"No, no, it's fine."

A teenager walked past with a dog, and I pretended to check my phone. This was the moment I needed a little divine inspiration, and when I glanced towards the sky, by some miracle, I got it. An open balcony door on the third floor, and the window next to it was steamed up. Somebody was in the shower, and since all the units on that floor were one-bedroom, the odds of being able to shortcut through their apartment unnoticed were reasonable.

Look left, look right, check behind me... Dusk had fallen, and my dark clothing didn't stand out in the gloom. A person in the building opposite walked past a brightly lit window, and I paused just in case until the coast was clear. Then I took a run up and leapt. If there was one thing I was good at, it was climbing buildings. I swarmed up rock faces in my spare time, what little I had of it, and I'd started doing parkour before the hipsters took over. Getting to the target balcony took me less than twenty seconds, and I waited outside, listening to the sounds of the apartment. An air conditioner. The TV playing quietly in one corner. Running water. And a dude singing an old Frank Sinatra song really, really badly. Forty seconds, and I'd scuttled to the front door. It clicked quietly behind me as I let myself out into the hallway.

Now where?

"I'm in. How far out is Snow?"

"Two minutes," Logan said. He'd been on the Special Projects team for the last six years, and I'd tasked him with tailing our bait tonight. "Perkins just turned into the parking lot."

Next question—what floor would they be going to? I ducked into a stairwell as the rush of adrenaline that came with my slightly unorthodox entrance subsided. From my hiding place, I could see the number panel next to the elevator, and a moment after Logan announced our target was in the building, the elevator rose swiftly. Two, three, four... Fuck, it wasn't stopping. No, it carried on going all the way to the fifteenth floor, which meant I needed to run. Fast.

I sprinted up the stairs, sucking in air as I neared the top. My thighs were on fire when I got into the fifteenth-floor hallway, but the only sign of Snow was the faint aroma of the perfume Bradley had doused her with before we left home. At least, until the glint of metal caught my eye and I spotted a gaudy gold bracelet on the floor outside apartment 1504.

Got her.

"Did anyone see where Perkins went?" I whispered into my radio.

"He just came back down in the elevator," Logan told me. Evidently, he'd found a spot where he could see in through the building's glass doors. "He's sitting in the lobby with a book. Looks prepared for a wait."

"Good. I'm going in. Unit 1504," I added, just in case the shit hit the fan and somebody needed to retrieve the bodies.

Today, I opted to use traditional lock picks rather than a bump key or a pick gun because silence was more important than speed. I listened for a moment before I started, grateful that this was the most boring apartment building ever and none of the neighbours were arguing or working out or listening to loud music. There was nothing except the faint sound of voices coming from my left. Snow talking to Clements—I recognised her speech patterns if not the Texan drawl she'd adopted for today's charade.

Apply pressure to the tension wrench, insert the pick... I'd learned to do this as a teenager when I needed to steal to eat. Shit, the elevator was on the move again. I sent a silent plea for it not to stop on this floor, but it was getting awfully close. Twelve, thirteen, fourteen...

I cracked the door open. For once, I wasn't worried about getting unexpectedly shot, which was kind of nice, but the prospect of being caught red-handed doing something reasonably illegal stopped me from enjoying the moment.

Clements was to my left, but luckily, Snow spotted me and showed the true meaning of taking one for the team by kissing him. Yeuch—he actually slurped. But her distraction gave me time to slip into the bedroom, complete with my backpack full of goodies. So far, so good.

I'd brought half a dozen tiny cameras that would transmit to Nate, who by now should be parked outside with his laptop. We had a vehicle just for that purpose. From the outside, it looked like a builder's van, complete with a ladder on the roof and the appropriate dents, but inside, he'd kitted it out with enough electronics to give Best Buy a wet dream.

The camera batteries would only last for twelve hours, but that was plenty of time for our purposes. Once we had what we needed, I'd sneak back in and retrieve our kit while Mack edited the footage for Clements's media firestorm.

But first, I had to find a good place to hide the cameras, and this apartment was devoid of the usual prime spots. No vases of flowers. No boxes of trinkets. No pictures on the walls or laundry hamper or TV. I eyed up the light fitting, but it was just a bare bulb hanging from the ceiling. An electrical socket? I'd brought a screwdriver, but did I have enough time to—

Fuck. Voices, and coming this way.

"I'm yours all night. Why don't we have a drink first?" Snow asked.

"I can't wait to have you. Heidi getting sick has turned into my lucky day."

A *thump* told me Snow had slammed Clements against a wall, and there was more fucking slurping as I looked around for a place to hide. The bed sat about two inches off the floor, which left a door on the opposite side of the room. I hoped for a bathroom, but as footsteps came in my direction, I found myself in a closet. A closet designed by a person with no concept of using space efficiently because the door opened inwards. Good grief—now I sounded like Bradley. Worse, when I pushed the door closed, the lock gave an ominous *click* I didn't like at all.

But at least it had a keyhole. I didn't know what paranoia had led somebody to put a lock on their damn closet, but as I threaded the flexible eye of one of Nate's cameras through to capture the action, I didn't particularly care either.

The slurping turned into squelching, and I felt like a bitch for putting Snow through this. Nate's voice in my ear confirmed it was every bit as bad as I thought.

"Someone better have alcohol waiting when Snow gets back."

"Why?" Mack asked. "To erase the memory of sleeping with an oversized maggot?"

"No, to wash out her—"

I didn't hear the rest because Snow spoke from a few feet away. "Shit."

What? What was wrong? That didn't sound like an in-character comment.

"Whoa," Nate said. "Is he...?"

Was he what? Did we have a problem?

CHAPTER 7

I PULLED THE camera out of the keyhole and pressed my face against the door so I could peer through. Snow was half-naked, still astride Clements, whose head lolled listlessly to the side.

"What's wrong?" I asked.

"He just..." A pause. "Great. He doesn't have a pulse."

Shit, shit, shit indeed. I wanted to help, but when I tried to pull the door open, the fucking handle came off in my gloved hand.

"And I'm stuck in the bloody closet."

Snow's head jerked in my direction. "You're what?"

When I turned a flashlight on, the mangled remains of the door spindle glinted back at me. I tried to slot the handle back on to turn it, but the mechanism was jammed.

"I'm stuck."

A snort of laughter came from the other side of the door.

"It's not fucking funny."

"What should I do about Clements? Start CPR? Call an ambulance? Leave him and pretend I was never here?"

The closet might have been small, but Mr. Murphy was wedged in there with me. "What happened? Did he have a heart attack?"

"Who knows? It was quick. Maybe an aneurysm burst or something?"

If that was the case, CPR wasn't going to cut it, and even if the congressman got to a hospital pretty sharpish, the chances were he wouldn't pull through. Perhaps karma had finally caught up with him? Whatever, it meant we needed to start damage control.

"Forget the first aid. Can you get me out of here?"

The door rattled from the outside but stayed firmly closed.

"You're right. It's stuck." The thick wood muffled Snow's voice, then a *thump* told me she'd tried to shoulder the door open. "And solid."

Normally, Nate would have been laughing his head off in a situation like this, but he seemed to have adopted a policy of radio silence, and that worried me as much as my current predicament. Maybe more.

"Nate? Did you hear what happened?"

"I heard, but we've got another issue here."

"What issue?"

"Don't worry; we're handling it."

A chill ran through me. Nate glossing over the details in that manner told me it was bad, and since dealing with bad was my speciality, his response meant only one thing. A problem with the man I cared about most. The last time Nate had acted all weird like this was three years ago, when my husband got into a knife fight in Chicago and came back with his arm in a sling. Knives were nasty things—if the blades came out, escaping unscathed was unlikely.

"Nate..." My voice rose an octave, and I forced it back under control. "Tell me what's going on."

"Just a few stray bullets. Focus on your job."

Focus? *Focus*? How did that asshole stay so calm? Sure, on the outside I always looked serene, but at times like this, my heart punched against my ribcage while my stomach did backflips.

I imagined my husband's voice in my head. *Take a step back, Diamond. Look at the problem objectively.*

Dammit, Nate was right, even if I'd never admit to that. I was trapped in the dark in a three-by-five-feet cupboard with a dead dude in the room outside, and succumbing to stress wouldn't get me out of there. Okay, I'd been in worse positions. At least nothing was on fire.

"Fine, I'll focus. Will you go and help the others?"

Nate's voice softened a smidgen. "On my way."

"Take Mack too, and whoever else you need. We'll be fine here."

Could I break out through the ceiling? I braced my back and shoulders off one wall and used my feet to walk up the one opposite. Nope, the ceiling was surprisingly solid. Flashlight between my teeth, I was about to try the walls when the beam bounced off something shiny. Bingo.

"I'm gonna take the hinge pins out. Start making this look like natural causes, yeah?"

Which technically it was, but who would believe that? The irony wasn't lost on me.

The hinges were stiff, but desperation helped me to lever the pins out with my screwdriver. When I got back into the bedroom, Snow was dressed, and the esteemed Mr. Clements was lying on the floor beside the bed with one leg in his trousers and his flaccid dick flopping over one thigh.

"I've wiped everything I touched," Snow said. "What's up? Never seen a dead body before?"

"Something's gone wrong on another job. Nate won't tell me what."

"Is it...?"

"I think so, yes."

"Fuck." Snow gave me a tight hug, which wouldn't have done my reputation much good if anyone else had seen, but having the breath squeezed out of me helped to squash down a little of the tension too. "He'll be okay. He always is. But I need you to give me a hand with getting this prick back into his clothes because he's not being very cooperative."

She wasn't wrong there. Even in death, Clements was an awkward fucker. Ever tried to stuff a giant squid into business attire? Me neither, but this was what I imagined it would be like. Worse, his sphincter muscles had loosened, and bodily fluids leaked all over the cheap carpet.

"I'm gonna puke." The stink clawed its way into my throat and wreaked havoc on my already delicate stomach. "How do undertakers do this every day?"

"I guess their olfactory receptors just give up. Better get those hinge pins back in now."

Between the pair of us, we rehung the door, and Snow touched up her make-up while I packed away the camera and removed any other evidence of my presence. On the bright side, we'd get a new congressman now, hopefully one who might serve the people of Virginia rather than himself.

"Ready to go?" I asked.

Snow nodded. She'd hitch a ride to the parking garage with Perkins as if everything were fine and the congressman hadn't carked it mid-fuck, then double back to collect me. When I got outside—taking the fire exit like a normal person this time—I started walking in Snow's direction. Anything to speed things along.

"Nate, we're out. Now tell me what the hell's going on."

Half an hour had passed since the first hint of a problem, but it felt like a lifetime.

"Everyone's clear. No serious damage to our people."

Thank goodness. The nervous energy that had kept me going left in a rush, and I stumbled on the sidewalk like a lousy drunk.

"What happened?"

"The team was waiting to go into the crack house when a gang turned up and started shooting. Not at us, but our job was to get the girl out of there alive rather than in a body bag."

"So we went in?"

"All guns blazing."

"And?"

"The score was Blackwood five, scumbags nil."

"Where is everyone now?"

"Our guys are at the hospital, the four prisoners are being booked into jail, and the dead fucker's probably in a body bag."

"The hospital? I thought you said there wasn't any serious damage?"

"There were a few cuts that needed patching up, and the cops are pissed."

Nothing new there. We had a love/hate relationship with the Richmond PD. The boots on the ground were happy when we solved problems they couldn't, and tended to turn a blind eye to a little rule-breaking every now and then. But the top brass hated us for making them look bad and creating mountains of the paperwork they seemed so obsessed with.

"We'll go straight there. And Nate?"

"Yes?"

"Don't keep things from me again."

"If I'd given you minute-by-minute updates, that would have put your operation in jeopardy. Nobody works well with that sort of distraction."

"So you were trying to help me?"

"Exactly."

"Well, next time don't bother. I can look after myself, and I don't appreciate being left in the dark."

"You live in the dark. I'll see you later."

The channel went dead, and I cursed under my breath. Was Nate right? Was it better to withhold bad news to protect somebody?

I hoped I'd never have to make that decision myself.

CHAPTER 8

NATE WAS AN asshole. No serious damage, he said, but my husband was lying in a hospital cubicle with a row of stitches in his thigh. Half an inch to the left, and the bullet would have nicked his femoral artery. I sat beside the bed, plotting murder until the doctor left and I found out the culprit was already in the morgue.

"Diamond, it's a hazardous job. We both know that."

I bit my tongue, literally, because what I really wanted to suggest was quitting and running off to a tropical island somewhere, far away from death and danger and morons who preyed on the innocent. An ex-boyfriend of mine had disappeared four years ago—just vanished—and although the circumstances had been somewhat awkward, in a strange way, I envied him his freedom. No ties, no responsibilities—he'd just left me a note and taken off in the middle of the night. Poof. Gone. I couldn't find him, and believe me I'd tried. I'd even roped Mack and Dan into helping me. On the quiet, of course, because although I secretly missed him, there was a teensy bit of animosity between him and my husband.

But now blood pooled in my mouth as I hung onto the words I didn't dare to say. "Yes, I know it's hazardous."

"It was only a ricochet."

"That doesn't make it better."

"The girl went home to her parents tonight. That makes it better."

"But—"

"What we do helps to make the world a safer place. We fight for what's right, and if that means the occasional injury, it's a price worth paying. Nobody lives forever, anyway."

"Even so—"

"And what else would we do? Sit on a beach somewhere? We'd be bored out of our fucking minds."

I tried for a smile, but it came out as more of a scowl. "I suppose."

"Let's go home. Dan wanted Chinese, right?"

There was a slight logistical problem with that idea. "What happened to your trousers?"

"The nurse cut them off."

I'd been trying not to stare, but I finally gave in and studied his legs. The blood-encrusted wound marred his left thigh, but I seized the opportunity to look past the damage to what lay underneath. Golden skin, solid muscles, the thick bulge of...

My reverie was interrupted by the doctor tugging the curtain back and clearing his throat.

"Uh, I brought these." He held up a pair of green drawstring trousers, the kind hospital staff wore. Looked from them to the man on the bed and back again. "On second thought, they might be a bit small."

"Forget it. Diamond, just pull the car up to the fire escape, and I'll go like this."

"Sir, you can't leave through the fire escape unless there's a fire."

"You'd rather I walked through the waiting area in my underwear?"

The doctor gulped and backed away. "I guess we could call it a drill or something." A nurse appeared and whispered something in the doctor's ear, and he nodded. "Excuse me—we have an emergency."

A cop tried to stop us as we left, but we stared him down, and he tripped over his own feet.

"Mr. Black, you can't leave. I have questions I need to ask."

"Not now. Call me tomorrow."

"But the captain—"

"Get him to call me tomorrow."

We left the officer behind, and I punched the bar on the fire exit and breathed in the cool night air. Fuck, I hated hospitals. Nothing good ever happened in those giant boxes of death and despair. And don't try to talk to me about the joy of childbirth, because kids scared the shit out of me.

Just like the rest of us, Snow preferred to keep out of the public eye, so she'd gone to ditch her stolen Toyota while I came inside to find my husband. When I phoned, she appeared in one of the Ford Explorers we used as pool cars, and we climbed into the back seat.

"Nice outfit." She turned to peer at his leg. If anyone else had done that, I'd have been tempted to poke their eyes out, but Snow was different. "Ouch."

"It's nothing."

"How many stitches?"

"Seventeen. Just drive."

As we turned onto the main road, an ambulance sped past, lights flashing and siren wailing, followed by two police cars and a guy on a motorbike with a camera slung over his shoulder.

"Reckon they've found Clements already?" I asked.

Snow smiled in the rear-view mirror. "Sure looks that way."

CHAPTER 9

AN HOUR AND a half later, I'd taken a Silkwood shower, got dressed in a comfortable pair of sweats, and curled up next to my husband on the sofa. The whole team had come back to our place, and yes, we had a Chinese feast, albeit from the cheap place that stayed open until the early hours rather than the fancy restaurant that served the tastiest satay chicken. Bradley had done his best to make it more palatable by handing out bottles of soy sauce and getting out the fancy chopsticks I'd brought back from a visit to Beijing last year.

The news played on the TV in the corner of the room, and while the anchor's words were sombre, his face said *holy hell, I can't believe this is happening.*

"Sources say the man found dead in an empty apartment earlier this evening was none other than Congressman Paul Clements, a man who's proven no stranger to controversy over the past year with his efforts to free the financial sector from regulation and those shocking comments he was caught making at the children's hospital last Christmas."

Ah yes, that moment he got taped moaning to his assistant about having to hand out gifts instead of playing golf, and the touching suggestion that it would be cheaper to let most of the kids die anyway. It *had* been him arriving at the hospital earlier as we left, but I doubted the medical staff had put too much effort into trying to revive him.

"So what happened?" Dan waved her chopsticks at Snow. "Come on, I want all the juicy details."

"There's really not much to tell. He just kinda... faded. Lights out."

"Has that ever happened before?"

"Nuh-uh. Usually, I have to give them a little helping hand. Potassium chloride or succinylcholine. Or sometimes an air embolism. Him just dying like that was creepy."

"Creepy?" I choked out a laugh, and Snow glared at me. "Sorry. But creepy is that guy I shot in Houston whose feet kept moving for a full five minutes after he breathed his last. Spring roll?"

"Thanks. Can somebody pass the sweet chilli sauce?"

"What're you gonna tell the widow?" Nate asked.

Dan shrugged. "Thought I'd play it by ear. See how happy she seems before I start on the details. If she's upset, I'll give her the sanitised pictures and tell her he was fine when we left. If she breaks out the champagne, I might mention he popped his clogs in flagrante delicto."

My money was on the champagne. "Reckon she'll need more 'therapy'?"

"A hundred bucks says she'll need full-time help."

"Babe, I'm not taking that bet."

The news anchor was still talking. "According to Edwin Perkins, Representative Clements's assistant, the apartment building downtown where Mr. Clements was found was one of many in his investment portfolio, and this evening's visit was a regular, pre-scheduled inspection. Nobody reports hearing anything untoward, and right now, there's no indication of foul play. We'll go over to Marcia, who's on the scene at the moment. Marcia, what can you tell us?"

Marcia couldn't tell anybody anything, because Marcia was a vapid blonde who could barely read an autocue. Still, she looked pretty, and that was all that mattered on TV nowadays. I tuned her out and dug into my prawn crackers again. Lucky my nutritionist went to bed at nine p.m. every night, because he'd have thrown a fit if he'd seen what I was eating. As well as the deep-fried crackers, the crispy shredded beef was swimming in grease, but it tasted good so I didn't care.

My husband stuck with sweet-and-sour chicken and steamed rice, and worse, he'd put on clothes now. No socks, no shoes. The casual look, even though he was anything but relaxed. He'd taken a couple of Advil earlier, and though he'd never admit to being in pain, the way he sat with his weight shifted to one side told me the truth.

"Are you okay?" I whispered.

He didn't answer, just put his half-empty carton of food back on the coffee table and stood up.

"I've got an early meeting."

Liar. I'd seen his schedule. But I stood with him anyway.

"And Alex is coming for me at six thirty, so I'm gonna turn in too."

Bradley gasped. "But we have Maotai and fortune cookies."

"Maotai?" The number-one brand of baijiu, China's favourite alcohol, which ranged from kinda spicy to pure fucking fire. Drink a shot of that at full strength, and the initial numbness was followed by panic and a desperate search for something, anything, that might help in removing it from your system. They didn't call it the white devil for nothing. "Then I'm definitely going to bed."

"Spoilsport." Bradley tossed a handful of fortune cookies in our direction. "At least eat these before you go."

I really didn't want to, but my husband unwrapped one, so I had little choice but to follow suit.

"Well?" Bradley asked.

I unfurled the tiny piece of paper. "Big changes lie ahead."

"And yours?" he asked my husband.

"The same."

"Well, that's boring." Bradley came over to check we weren't fibbing. "What kind of cheap-ass cookies are these? Here, have another one."

"We're going to bed."

Bradley's protests continued, but we ignored him as we headed for the stairs. Even with stitches, my husband refused to use the elevator.

"You didn't answer my question," I said.

"What question?"

"Are you okay?"

He stayed silent the whole way to the second floor where our bedrooms were. He still hadn't answered when I followed him into his.

"You're not okay?"

Still nothing, but he tugged off his shirt and threw it into the laundry hamper. "Just had a taste of my own mortality today, that's all."

"But earlier, you said—"

"I know what I said." He stepped closer, so close I had to tip my head back to meet his gaze. Heat rushed through me, and I couldn't even blame it on the baijiu. "But what I said and how I feel are two different things."

"So how do you feel?"

"There are so many things left I want to do, and I don't want to run out of time to do them."

"Like what?"

He cupped my cheek in his palm, and I leaned into his touch.

"I'll keep that to myself for now. Get some sleep, Diamond. You're not skipping a session with Alex just because you took a door off its hinges."

"Asshole."

The man I loved laughed and turned away. "Yes. Yes, I am."

CHAPTER 10

THE PRELIMINARY AUTOPSY report came in just before I left for the airport with Snow. Unofficial, of course, but we had sources at the hospital. Mr. Clements had died from a heart attack followed by sudden cardiac arrest. The news today had been full of politicians giving their condolences, including my ex, who'd said all the right words then sent me a smiley face afterwards using a burner phone he wasn't supposed to have. And following our meeting this morning when she'd been remarkably chipper, Rhonda Swanson had donned a black outfit and done a convincingly heartfelt interview, including tears and a pledge to donate money to the children's wing of the hospital in her husband's memory. Nice touch, lady. She'd also couriered over a crate of Veuve Clicquot and the mother of all fruit baskets, so at least I had something to look forward to when I got home.

"Where are you off to?" I asked Snow as we climbed into the car. She always travelled light, and her single suitcase contained almost everything she owned. I say *almost* because she kept a bunch of stuff she didn't want people to see in a storage room in our basement.

"South America. Argentina to start off with. I've taken a long contract, so I won't be back for a while. But I'll call."

"I'm not going anywhere."

"Sure you're not tempted by a vacation?"

"I've got everything I need at home."

If only I'd known what lay ahead, perhaps I'd have gone with her. Climbed onto the plane and flown to a far-off land where pain couldn't touch me. Found a new sanctuary. But I didn't, so when we arrived at Dulles International, I just leaned over and hugged her. Kissed her for old times' sake.

"Let me know if you need anything?"

She gave my hand one last squeeze. "You'll always be the first person I call."

It wouldn't be long before I'd make the journey to Dulles again, but with my heart broken and agony seeping out of every pore. Karma was a bitch, almost as much of a bitch as me. Maybe I should have guessed what fate had in store for me, but that day, as Snow wheeled her plain black suitcase towards the terminal, I put the car in gear and turned towards Richmond.

For now, I'd live in ignorant bliss, or as close to it as I could manage.

What's next?

Diamond

Diamond's life unravels over the first three books in the Blackwood Security series, starting with Pitch Black. Will her fortune change for the better or the worse?

The Black Trilogy: Pitch Black - Into the Black - Forever Black

After the owner of a security company is murdered, his sharp-edged wife goes on the run. Forced to abandon everything she holds dear—her home, her friends, her job in special ops—assassin Diamond builds a new life for herself in England. As Ashlyn Hale, she meets Luke, a handsome local who makes her realise just how lonely she is.

Yet, even in the sleepy village of Lower Foxford, the dark side of life dogs Diamond's trail when the unthinkable strikes. Forced out of hiding, she races against time to save those she cares about.

With her husband's killer still on the loose and her life in England a disaster, Diamond returns to the only thing she knows: work. As the star of Blackwood Security takes on enemies from the States to Syria, she finds the toughest battle is the one going on in her own head.

Her training has equipped her to handle the most dangerous situations, but controlling her own emotions isn't so easy. All she wants is justice, but can she mend her broken heart as well?

Pitch Black is available to read **FREE**:
www.elise-noble.com/pitch-black

Save money on all three books with a box set:
www.elise-noble.com/box-sets

Snow

Snow's story is told in the first three books of the Blackwood Elements series, starting with Oxygen. In terms of timescale, Oxygen starts after book three in the Blackwood Security series, Forever Black, so if you want to read about both girls, I'd suggest starting with Diamond's story first.

Blackwood Elements: Oxygen - Lithium - Carbon

When tragedy strikes, Akari Takeda moves to Boston with her young son to follow her dream of becoming a pianist. But three men get in her way—Jansen, the skilled but uptight violinist, easygoing Jude, who understands how important coffee is to a girl, and Lincoln, the smooth-talking janitor who looks good in leather.Which of them will steal her heart, and who isn't everything he seems?

After clearing up the mess in Boston, assassin Snow wants a fresh start of her own. But first, she needs to take a trip to paradise to give her ex what he deserves. That should be straightforward for a woman with her skills, but she's not the only one who wants Raul dead, and newcomer Leo threatens to derail her plans in more ways than one.

Meanwhile, in England, novelist Augusta Fordham's got a problem of her own, or rather, two of them. Caught between wealthy doctor Gregory and a dark stranger who makes her pulse race as he indulges her fantasies, will she choose comfort and security or take a leap into the unknown?

When she makes her decision, she's thrust into a

world of secrets and lies with no one to trust. Only Emmy, her new flatmate, seems to be on Augusta's side as she discovers there's just one truth: love is never easy.

For more details:
www.elise-noble.com/oxygen

Save money on all three books with a box set:
www.elise-noble.com/box-sets

While this prequel is a short novella, the other books are full-length novels.

Want to stalk me?

For updates on my new releases, giveaways, and other random stuff, you can sign up for my newsletter on my website:
www.elise-noble.com

Facebook:
www.facebook.com/EliseNobleAuthor

Twitter: @EliseANoble

Instagram: @elise_noble

If you're on Facebook, you may also like to join Team Blackwood for exclusive giveaways, sneak previews, and book-related chat. Be the first to find out about new stories, and you might even see your name or one of your ideas make it into print!

And if you'd like to read my books for FREE, you can also find details of how to join my advance review team.

Would you like to join Team Blackwood?

www.elise-noble.com/team-blackwood

OTHER BOOKS BY ELISE NOBLE

The Blackwood Security Series
For the Love of Animals (Nate & Carmen - prequel)
Black is my Heart (Diamond & Snow - prequel)
Pitch Black
Into the Black
Forever Black
Gold Rush
Gray is my Heart
Neon (novella)
Out of the Blue
Ultraviolet
Glitter (novella)
Red Alert
White Hot
Sphere (novella)
The Scarlet Affair
Spirit (novella) (2020)
Quicksilver
The Girl with the Emerald Ring (2020)
Red After Dark (2020)
When the Shadows Fall (2020)

The Blackwood Elements Series
Oxygen
Lithium

Carbon
Rhodium
Platinum
Lead
Copper
Bronze
Nickel
Hydrogen (TBA)

The Blackwood UK Series
Joker in the Pack
Cherry on Top (novella)
Roses are Dead
Shallow Graves
Indigo Rain
Pass the Parcel (TBA)

Blackwood Casefiles
Stolen Hearts

Blackstone House
Hard Lines (2021)
Hard Tide (TBA)

The Electi Series
Cursed
Spooked
Possessed
Demented
Judged (2021)

The Trouble Series
Trouble in Paradise

Nothing but Trouble
24 Hours of Trouble

Standalone
Life
Coco du Ciel (TBA)
Twisted (short stories)
A Very Happy Christmas (novella)

Books with clean versions available (no swearing and no on-the-page sex)
Pitch Black
Into the Black
Forever Black
Gold Rush
Gray is my Heart

Audiobooks
Black is my Heart (Diamond & Snow - prequel)
Pitch Black
Into the Black
Forever Black
Gold Rush

www.ingramcontent.com/pod-product-compliance
Lightning Source LLC
Chambersburg PA
CBHW020648130626
46552CB00003B/1443